THE GOOD BAD CAT

Written by
Nancy Antle
Illustrated by
John Sandford

The cat ran under the chair.

“Bad cat!”

The cat ran over the game.

“Bad cat!”

The cat jumped on the table.

"Bad cat!"

The cat saw a mouse.

So did everyone else.

The mouse ran under the chair,
over the game,
and across the table.

So did the cat.

The mouse ran out of the house.

The cat did not.

“Good cat!”

"Good cat!"